The Misadventures of Harry and Larry

Path of the Way Show-ers

2

Printed in Australia

Cover design by Shawline Publishing Group Pty Ltd
Images in this book are the copyright of Shawline
Publishing Group
Illustrations within this book are the copyright of
Shawline Publishing Group

First Printing: 2022

Shawline Publishing Group Pty Ltd

www.shawlinepublishing.com.au

Paperback ISBN- 9781922701954

Ebook ISBN- 9781922751058

A catalogue record for this
book is available from the
National Library of Australia

DAVID WEBBY

The Misadventures of Harry and Larry

Path of the Way Show-ers

2

MER D'ARAFOURA
I. Melville
I. Bathurst
Dét d'End
G. de Van Diemen
C. Arnheim
Darwin
Tre d'Arnheim
GOLFE D
CARPENTAR
...OR
AUSTRALIA
Roper Fl.
Tomato Island
Mataranka
Butterfly Spring
Télégraphe
Victoria R.
Southern Lo.
Borroloo
L. Woods
Monts
Ashburton
Burketown
TERRE
Liechard F.
Lac
Mt Wilson
ALEXANDRA
g.
White
Spring
Lac
Désert sablonneux
Marie Spring
Mt Farewell
ésert
Waterloo Spring
Mt Stuart Central
QUE
Eva Spring
Mt Stanley
du
Monts
Mac Donnell
Alice Spring
onneux
Désert pierreux
Végétation
nulle
E
Diamentina
AUSTRALIE
Warburton R.
Cooper R.
Lac Eyre
LE
Mts Stuart
Farina Tow
MÉRIDIONALE
Stuart Creek

140
150
10
e Torres
squ'ile
York
Nouvelle
Guinée
Archipel de la
Louisiade
MER DE CORAIL
GRAND OCEAN
PACIFIQUE
C. Melville
C. Flattery
Cooktown
Mitchell R.
manton
119
Palm Cove
Cairns
Undarra
Volcano NP
Townsville
Great Barrier Ref
Hughenden
Mackay
20
NSLAND
Clermont
ricorne
rcaldine Dns
son R.
Rockhampton
Bundaberg
C. Sandy
I. Frazer
Charleville
Gympie
Paroo R.
Warrego R.
Balonne R.
Barwon R.
Brisbane
Gold Coast
es Bleues

To my brother Brian

*Your passion and enthusiasm for life and love of music, food,
and hiking, made an everlasting impact upon my life.*

This one's for you

Acknowledgements:

Thanks to Justy and Margaret, who planned and orchestrated 'The People's Library', that inspired me to finish writing this series of adventures

BOOK 2:

Path of the Way Show-ers

Recap from Book 1:

Chapter 1: The Way Show–ers

Chapter 2: Anyone for Steak?

Chapter 3: The Balance of Life

Chapter 4: The Road less Travelled

Chapter 5: Lost City

Chapter 6: The Monster of Butterfly Springs

Chapter 7: Croc Country

Chapter 8: A Magical Journey

Recap From
Book One
★

Harry and Larry are twin Mice brothers, who lived with their Mama and Papa, three sisters, and two older brothers in a small mousey cottage deep in the rainforest of the Bunya Mountains National Park.

However, the two Mice brothers didn't conform to the usual training of the Mouse household. They considered themselves brave Mouseketeers– Adventurers– and couldn't resist the temptations that lay beyond the boundaries of their Mousey house. Mama Mouse said they were always poking their noses into everything and warned them that one day their noses would get them into trouble.

On the hunt for delicious treasures, the two Mice found themselves trapped in Charlie and Izzy Humbledinks's Toyota 4WD and transported to the Gold Coast. Harry and Larry thought their adventures had come to an end after been cornered by Princess Molly the Cat and Scratch the Dog, guardians of the Humbledink's household. So, Harry and Larry launched an ingenious ambush, battering them with water bombs, toothpick catapults, almond oil and confetti.

Charlie and Izzy were surprised by the Mice's successful ambush and were shocked when they discovered that Harry and Larry could communicate with human speak. They invited the boys on a camping holiday, an adventure to explore Queensland and beyond. Larry was thrilled as he had read about many amazing places across Australia, on Mrs Google, and was keen to experience the red, red, soil of the Outback.

Harry and Larry were quick to show their camping skills, learnt from Mouse Scouts, which certainly got Charlie out of a few disasters that he brought upon himself. One can't forget the incident of the fire in the camper trailer and the soggy mattress when they were caught in heavy rain at Mission Beach. Charlie added his own version of gymnastics when strangled by a 'Wait-a-While' vine whilst hiking on Dunk Island. Where there's trouble, Charlie Humbledink is usually at the centre of it.

Charlie Humbledink is often called a 'lovable duffer' by his wife Izzy. However, her patience wears thin when Charlie gets flustered or makes mistakes. Although Mrs H has a short fuse, she is a very kind-hearted person and loves animals. Izzy also has many talents, including sewing, and has won many awards from the Country Women's Association for her knitting and crocheted handicrafts. Much to Harry and Larry's delight, she sewed two little side pouches on Charlie's backpack for when they go hiking. She also made little safari outfits for the boys, much to the amusement of some of the Red-tailed Black Cockatoos.

Thanks to the help of the Cockatoo Telegraph, their Mis-Adventures become legendary, particularly after the predictions foretold by Wilmar, Queen Mother of the great Humpback Whales. During a boat trip near Fraser Island, the Mice met up with Wilmar, who took them on a journey back in time from the beginning of Gondwana land through to the future of Mother Earth. She told them they may be the Chosen Ones, as foreseen in the Prophecy: to help Humans reconnect with Nature and the Animal Kingdom. Such a title, bestowed on simple bush Mice, was a great shock, and Harry and Larry were dumfounded to say the least.

Black Jack, the leader of a flock of Red-tailed Black Cockatoos, took them on a scenic flight of the Great Barrier Reef. The Mice learned about the fragility of the Great Barrier Reef and its decline. Both Harry and Larry were overwhelmed by the possible demise of Mother Earth, particularly if humans aren't able to evolve with the wisdom of the ages. Black Jack reassured them not to worry about what they can't achieve, but to be the small changes they can.

During an adventure to explore the Daintree rainforests, the Mice met up with a friendly Cassowary called Corey, who earned his keep by scaring the tourists from bus tours. When he learned the Mice were the legendary Chosen Ones, he took them to see a splendid view of the Daintree and asked them to save the Daintree and its inhabitants from decline caused by human expansion into their rainforests.

The Mice were overwhelmed by the expectations placed upon them to suddenly change the world. Mr H shared with the Mice the awareness and happiness the Mice have brought into his life and reassured them to take one step at a time.

With the predictions shown to them by Wilmar the Queen Mother Whale, who said they were here to help in some way, their destiny may become clearer with time. Who knows who they will meet and the challenges they will face during their next Mis-Adventure.

And so, the journey continues ...

CHAPTER ONE

The Way Show-ers

★

'Good evening,' said a Voice.

It was dark, despite the small solar lights indicating the pathways around the campsite. The sky was clear and moonless, without the glow from city lights. It was dark, because it was the outback.

Charlie and Izzy and the Mice brothers, Harry and Larry, were sitting around a campfire after a long day of driving. They had left the tropical beach oasis of Palm Cove, north of Cairns, and struggled up the steep winding road to the Atherton Tablelands with the heavy camper trailer in tow, onto the plateau of the Great Dividing Range. Further west they drove, past the giant red termite mounds near the hot springs around the town of Innot. Finally, they pulled into Undara National Park, just at dusk, the red and pink colours of the clouds turning grey.

They were all tired after the drive and putting up the tent in the dark wasn't much fun, but Mr H and the two Mice erected the tent in record time. An hour later they were relaxing with a cuppa around the fire, oblivious to the strange visitor hidden in the darkness.

'Cough, cough! Good evening, I said,' piped the Voice again.

Harry and Larry squinted into the shadows. They could make out a dark outline of a ...

'Mouse hunter!' cried Harry. 'Hide!'

'What? No! Run!' cried Larry.

They took off, but in their panic, they ran straight into each other. Bang! Their heads collided, pushing them backwards on to their bottoms, momentarily stunned.

'Ha, ha, ha, ha!' said the Voice. 'Good show! Do it again! Haven't had a good laugh for ages.'

'We're not very t–t–t–tasty,' stuttered Larry.

'I think you would be very tasty indeed,' laughed the Voice. 'You look very well fed, but very strange to see Mice in human clothes.'

'Mr and Mrs H look after us,' said Harry, 'in exchange for our talents.'

'Tasty and talented,' laughed the Voice. 'Starting to tickle my taste buds.'

'I'm not ready to d–d–die,' stuttered Larry.

'I don't think you have a say in that, Mousekins,' said the Voice. 'This wise old Owl knows that life in the outback can appear to be harsh and unkind. But it has a sense of order, where all things are in balance. One dies and gives life to another.'

Harry remembered their recent skirmish with the Sea Eagles chicks. He'd thought it was the end of their adventures, but luckily they were able to fight them off, and escape with the help of their Mousey sailor friends from Captain Cookson's ship. He looked around for some twigs to fight off this Mouse Catcher, but there were none in sight. It was down to a war of words, and if they lost, they would face death, once again.

'Stop right there! No one is going to gobble us up for dinner!' cried Harry, puffing out his chest. 'We're on a special mission. Both Black Jack the Cockatoo and Wilmar, Grandmother Whale, said we were the Chosen Ones, so you can't eat us!'

'Well, well,' replied the Owl. 'So, you're the little rascals! The Red-tailed Black Cockatoos spoke of your adventures many weeks ago. The Cockatoo Telegraph tells no lies. The talk of two Bush Mice travelling with their human caretakers, and their heroic deeds, has been front page chitter-chatter ever since.'

With that, the Owl flew down from the shadows to a tree stump near their camp.

Harry and Larry jumped back in surprise. Larry, still certain he was going to be the Owl's next meal, ducked behind his brother.

'Wow!' said Charlie. 'An Owl just flew into our campsite.'

'It's a sign.' said Izzy. 'Owls are said to represent great wisdom.'

'Greetings, Dear Ones,' said the Owl. 'I am Merlin the Wise.'

'Did you hear that?' said Charlie. 'I can hear him talking!'

'I heard it too!' said Izzy, looking very excited.

'Greetings, Sir Merlin,' said Harry. 'We are honoured to meet you. I am Harry and this is my brother Larry, sons of Mousolini Papa Mouse, leader of the Giant Stinging Tree clan, King of the Bunya tribes.'

'It is a great honour to finally meet you sirs, Harry and Larry,' replied Merlin. 'You do have a special role in life. There are a few special beings in life that think outside the box of normality. Innovators. Explorers. They help us adapt and change. They are the Way Show-ers.'

'Way Show-ers?' repeated Larry, feeling a little less nervous.

'Yes,' said Merlin. 'They shed light on new paths,

or sometimes old paths that have been forgotten.'

Harry remembered Black Jack's warning about the tragic demise of the Great Barrier Reef, and Corey the Cassowary's fear of human housing expansion adversely affecting the Daintree rainforest. Being told they were the Chosen Ones and now the Way Show-ers felt very overwhelming. Harry felt confused. 'But what is our role in all of this?' exclaimed Harry. 'We're just simple bush Mice.'

'The path will reveal itself when you are ready,' advised Merlin. 'Besides, there are certain Virtues you will need to understand before the Prophecy can be fully revealed to you.'

'What!' cried Harry. 'This is a never-ending journey of confusion!'

'Patience, young Harry,' said Merlin. 'A wise Owl doesn't become wise overnight. It takes time. May your journey open your mind and heart to the deeper connections of Life.'

Harry slumped down on his log seat. He didn't understand and wanted a simple answer from the

Owl, something to bring a little clarity to his mind.

'If it wasn't for our human friends, we wouldn't even be on this journey,' Larry told the Owl. 'Their names are Charlie and Izzy Humbledink, but we call them Mr and Mrs H.'

Suddenly Merlin flew across the fire pit and landed on Izzy's knees.

'Oh, my Goodness!' she cried, almost falling backwards out of her camp chair.

'Greetings, Dear Ones,' said Merlin. 'Your Mouse friends here speak fondly of you, and it is wonderful to note your participation in their great journey. It has been foreseen that one by one, humans will re-learn the old ways of communicating with the Animal Kingdom. I am deeply honoured to be a part of that, too.'

'The honour is mine, too!' exclaimed Izzy.

'I knew it! I knew they could talk,' rattled Charlie excitedly, jumping around on his seat.

'Yes, Charlie Humbledink,' said Merlin. 'We can talk, just as you can. But the point is that I can hear you, and you can hear me.'

'Y-yes, I-I-I hear you,' stuttered Charlie.

'That is the key,' said Merlin, 'in understanding the integration of Human and Animal Kingdoms. The willingness to listen.'

'I think I get it,' said Charlie, still in shock that he could hear the Owl talking to him.

'You will understand more in time,' said Merlin the Owl. 'So long, Mousketeers, Sir, Madam. Honoured to meet you all.'

And with that Merlin opened his giant wings and effortlessly flew away into the shadows of the night.

'Well I'll be …' said Charlie. 'A talking Owl!'

'More than that,' said Izzy. 'A Wisdom Keeper.'

Harry and Larry were chattering excitedly together.

'I wonder what Virtues he's talking about,' whispered Larry.

'And he told us that the Prophecy is going to be revealed to us,' Harry squeaked back. 'Can't wait!'

'He said we're the Way Show-ers,' said Larry.

'Don't let it go to your heads, boys,' said Charlie. 'Mrs H will soon pull the mat from under your feet.'

'So true,' laughed Izzy. 'Don't want your heads bursting from an inflated ego. And talking about Way Show-ers,' she added. 'Time to show you the way to bed. I think it's been a long day and there's a lot to digest.''

'Sure thing, Mrs H,' laughed Harry.

'Night, night,' laughed Larry.

And they scuttled off to their cosy beds.

Larry's did you know...

Undara Volcanic is a national park in North Queensland, Australia, 275 km from Cairns.

A massive eruption, occurring 190,000 years ago, causing hot magnum lava to be expelled over 1550 square kilometres of the Atherton Tablelands. It is estimated that 23 billion cubic meters of lava flowed from this volcano. One of the longest lava flows was 160km in length.

When the surrounding circumference of a lava flows solidify, it would form a lava tube.

Part of longest lava tube that remains today is called the Bayliss cave, and was once over 100 km in length.

The word *Undara* is Aboriginal in origin and means *a long way*.

CHAPTER TWO

Anyone for Steak?

★

Bump! Clang! Oops!

'What's that?' said Charlie bolting upright.

He tried looking out the window of the camper trailer, forgetting he'd zipped up the windows to protect them from the rain. The Humbledinks and Mice brothers had continued driving west across the vast grazing lands of Western Queensland, setting up camp on a secluded bush site.

'What's wrong?' mumbled Izzy drowsily.

'I think we have intruders,' whispered Larry.

'They're bumping around in the camp kitchen,' added Harry.

They heard a big slurp from outside. 'Mmmmmmmmm, not bad,' said a Voice.

'Oh no! my veggie soup,' cried Charlie. 'I left it out to cool!' He quickly zipped down the window and peered outside. He jumped, seeing two big brown eyes staring back.

'What do you think you're doing?' exclaimed Charlie, making out the form of a big Cow.

Chomp, chomp, gulp! The Cow looked up lazily. 'Eating, of course! That's what us Cows do!'

'But that's our dinner,' said Charlie.

'Mmmm, not bad,' said the Cow. 'I'm quite partial to veggie soup. Fragrances of parsley and carrot are nice, but you used too much onion and pepper. Slurp, slurp.'

'Hey! Who do you think you are?' said Charlie.

'What's up, Charlie Humbledink?' laughed Izzy. 'Is the Cow giving you a hard time?'

The Mice giggled.

'But, but ...' said Charlie, his voice becoming squeaky and high pitched. 'That Cow reckons my soup is not good enough!'

'What did you say?' asked the Cow, letting out a

giant burp. 'I'm actually enjoying this. Growing on me every minute.'

The Mice fell over backwards in laughter.

'I MEAN IT. STOP RIGHT THERE!' yelled a flustered Charlie, his face now red and spotty. 'One more drink and you'll be STEAK!'

Harry and Larry gasped.

'Charlie!' exclaimed Mrs Humbledink.

'OH NO! You're kidding me!' said the Cow. 'Now you've really hurt my feelings.'

Charlie took a deep breath and sighed. 'I'm sorry Mrs Cow. It just slipped out of my mouth, but that doesn't excuse you for eating my soup.'

'No apologies can excuse you from calling me Steak!' said the Cow. 'How would you feel if you were served up on a plate? Please sir, how do you like your human rump? Rare, medium or well done? See what I mean?'

Charlie heard Izzy gasp in the background.

'Well when you put it that way ... mmm, I do see your point,' said Charlie. 'But Cows aren't supposed to have emotions.'

'Who says Cows don't have emotions!' exclaimed the Cow. 'You weren't around when they dragged off my Aunt Bessie and Uncle Harold last week, mooing and bellowing. They loaded up a whole bunch of my relatives, and squashed them into a dusty old truck, destined for a Cow factory in some distant land.'

Izzy started to cry. Harry and Larry were gobsmacked.

'Do you humans have any compassion for the likes of us? Insensitive creatures!' exclaimed the Cow.

'But, but ...' said Charlie.

'Yeah right,' said the Cow. 'Bet you wouldn't call me Steak now! Eh buddy!'

Charlie was speechless. Izzy was wiping her red eyes. Harry and Larry were hiding in shame.

The Cow turned back towards the soup. 'Now where was I ... mmm ... soup.'

'Help yourself, Mrs Cow,' said Izzy. 'I don't think

we'll be having soup tonight.'

'Thank you, Madam,' said the Cow. 'I really love a good veggie soup. Can't say I've tasted better!'

'Looks like its baked beans tonight,' laughed Harry.

'That was one of my best soups,' moaned Charlie.

The Cow finished off the rest of the soup, let go another long burp and wandered off.

'It's not fair!' exclaimed Charlie. 'Merlin said I need to learn how to communicate with Animals, and what do I get? An emotional Cow who tells me I'm insensitive, and then eats all my soup!'

The Mice giggled.

'Well, you did ask for it, Honey Bun,' laughed Izzy. 'I guess you'll have to learn to share.'

Charlie grumbled under his breath, and headed out to their camp kitchen to make breakfast.

Larry's did you know...

The Gulf Savannah region has been occupied by indigenous Aboriginal people for over 50,000 years and in more contemporary times by pastoralists, fishermen and miners.

The Savannah Way was named in honour of the early explorers, surveyors and cattlemen who have travelled along this route which spans from Cairns to Broome and covers 3,700 km

German explorer, Ludwig Leichhardt, led an expedition from Brisbane to Darwin in 1844–45, where they travelled nearly 5000 km in just 14 months. They survived by living off bush tucker gathered by Aboriginal expedition members.

The telegraph line from Bowen to Burketown was surveyed in 1866 by Frederick Walker, only a few years after the ill-fated Burke and Wills expedition in 1861.

The discovery of gold, tin, zinc, copper and other metals, led to the establishment of little towns, starting with the Croydon gold rush in 1886.

From the 1872 drovers took thousands of cattle along what is now The Savannah Way to supply miners across the Gulf, and into the Northern Territory and Western Australia. Famous drover, Nat Buchanan, drove thousands of cattle across the 'Top Road,' now known as the Savannah Way.

CHAPTER THREE

The Balance of Life

★

'Gees, she's pretty rugged out here.' said Charlie.

They had just left Normanton and were heading along the red dirt road they called the Savannah Way, a rough outback highway celebrating the journeys of early explorers, gold diggers and cattlemen. The corrugations of the dirt road caused the windows of the 4WD to rattle noisily, the vibrations pulsing through the whole body of the vehicle. A huge red dust cloud billowed up behind them. Ahead, the vibrant red road disappeared into the distant blue sky. The land went on and on, forever.

The Mice were perched on the window ledge of the Toyota.

'I thought it was supposed to be tropical bush up

here in North Queensland,' said Harry.

'We are a fair way inland from the coastal mountains,' answered Larry. 'They don't get much rain up here in the dry season.'

'I guess so,' replied Harry, 'but I wouldn't like to be a Mouse in this land. Tough work to feed a family.'

'Is that a Bird up ahead?' cried Izzy.

'Not sure,' said Charlie. 'I guess we'll find out.'

As the Toyota lumbered closer, the giant Eagle stopped tearing at its dead prey, and spread its wings to fly off. The sunlight shone golden through the striped patterns of its feathers, as it lifted high into the sky.

'Wow! It's a Wedge-tail,' said Charlie.

Larry squirmed. The memory of the battle with the Sea Eagle chicks was fresh in his memory. Every time he saw a pair of sharp claws, his head started to spin.

As they passed the Wedge-tail's lifeless meal lying at the side of the road, Izzy said 'Bless you.'

'Lunch doesn't look too tasty,' said Charlie.

'That depends if you like sun-baked flesh and maggots,' laughed Harry.

'Ewwwwwww!' cried Larry.

Charlie kept a sharp eye on the road ahead, dodging pointy rocks and soft ruts of sand that could spell danger to unsuspecting travellers.

A cloud of dust appeared ahead in the far distance. 'I think we have visitors,' he said.

Five minutes later they recognised the outline of a large truck powering towards them, the huge cloud of dust engulfing the road and the bush on either side.

'Can't see a thing past that truck,' said Charlie.

'Maybe we should stop?' suggested Izzy.

'She'll be right,' answered Charlie. 'Can't be that bad.'

Suddenly the truck was upon them. It commanded the road and all that was upon it. A small dark figure sat behind the giant steering wheel.

'Wow!' said Harry. 'The sign on the front says Road Train. What's a ...'

Harry's voice was lost in the commotion of the rumbling tyres, as a huge cloud of red-brown dust swallowed them.

'Quick. The windows!' yelled Izzy.

Charlie scrambled for the electronic window controls but it was too late.

The 4WD was suddenly filled with dust, which caused everyone to cough and splutter. Charlie could only steer blindly into the abyss, trying not to drive off the road. Carriages full of cattle hurtled past them like pirate ships in the mist.

'One ... two ... three ... four ...' counted Harry. 'Four carriages!'

'That's a lot of Cows going to market,' said Larry. He thought about Mrs Cow who had drank Mr H's soup and her sad recollection of relatives who had been taken off for slaughter, maybe in similar Road Trains as this one.

'Crikey,' said Charlie, as he desperately peered through the blanket of dust. He braked to a slow stop, watching intently for the road. 'Golly gosh, that was huge!'

'Charlie Humbledink, you idiot!' exclaimed Izzy. 'Why didn't you close the windows, before it was too late?'

'Sorry, Izzy. But I was spellbound by the size of that thing. Can't say I want to meet one of those again in a hurry.'

'We'll be more prepared next time, won't we?' declared Izzy, glaring at Charlie.

'Yes, Darling,' he replied apologetically.

After several minutes, the dust finally cleared and they took off again, along the red, red road.

A little while later, a sign pointed to Camp 119.

'Hey, boys,' cried Charlie. 'Check this out. This is the northern-most campsite for Burke and Wills.'

'Oh, I've heard of them,' said Izzy. 'Silly blighters, took a bet to be the first ones to travel from the South to the North of Australia.'

'Not so silly,' said Charlie. 'Brave explorers they were. Pioneers of Australia!'

'Yeah, maybe,' said Izzy, 'the prize money is no good to you if you die trying.'

They pulled up to the campsite where there was an information board and a small monument to honour the two men and their party.

As Larry started to read the information board,

he imagined the sheer frustration and disbelief of Burke, Wills and King when they finally returned to camp 75, to find their support party had left only 9 hours before. He had once read on Mrs Google about this failed expedition, but to be here was like relieving the past. Tears welled up in Larry's eyes as he thought of their hopelessness and their subsequent death. He was surprised to read how young these humans were when they died. They too, were far from home. Would he and Harry return back to the Bunyas alive?

'Wills was only 27 and Burke was 40,' said Larry. 'They died of starvation and toxins from eating undercooked bush tucker.'

'Hooley Dooley!' said Charlie.

'Make sure you remember that, Charlie,' cautioned Izzy. 'Don't eat anything you don't know.'

'Course not,' exclaimed Charlie, as he headed back to the car for his camera.

Izzy walked off in the other direction towards a small stony creek, named Little Bynoe River. She loved collecting coloured stones from the creek beds.

The Mice explored around the trees where Burke had blazed fifteen trees to mark their campsite. On one of the trees, the Roman numerals B CXIX were carved out to indicate the number 119.

'This tree must be over 160 years old,' stated Harry as he knocked on the trunk.

'Hello,' spoke a Voice.

Harry jumped. 'Did you hear that?'

'Sure, I heard a voice,' said Larry. 'You sure it wasn't Mr H playing tricks on us?'

'Not this time. Besides he's way over there,' said Harry, looking towards Charlie, who was crouched on the ground taking photos of wild flowers.

The tree was silent. Only the cry of a Crow could be heard in the distance.

'Try again,' suggested Larry.

Harry knocked on the trunk of the tree again, three times.

'Who goes there?' said the Voice.

The Mice jumped.

'Who is rude enough to disturb my nap?' asked the Voice.

'It's only us,' squeaked the Mice, as they huddled together.

A wispy ghost appeared, rising from the roots of the tree. 'Ha,' said the Ghost. 'Two little bush Mice. Hardly worth a meal.'

'Please don't eat us,' pleaded Larry.

'Can't say I'm so hungry that I'll stoop to eating rodents,' said the Ghost. 'Although you would add some flavour to the soup.'

'We're just travelling through,' said Harry. 'Haven't time to stop for soup.'

'Too bad,' said the Ghost. 'So, you're not from around here?'

'No, S–s–sir,' stuttered Larry. 'We come from the Bunya Mountains.'

'Can't say I've heard of those,' replied the Ghost. 'Pretty flat country around here. Got to watch out for those boggy mangroves. Very disheartening, eh what?'

'By the way, who are you?' asked Harry.

'My name is William John Wills, official surveyor and navigator for the trans-Australian expedition. Call me Wills. My colleague and friend, Robert O'Hara Burke, is the leader of the Expedition. We are the first explorers to navigate from the south to the north of Australia. My mate, Burke, has just gone for a walk to see if he can find another way around the mangroves.'

'But didn't you die, back in 1861?' asked Larry.

'Can't be!' exclaimed Wills. 'Burke promised he was going to get us out of this mess. He said he would be back in a few hours.'

'Sorry mate,' said Harry. 'It's true. Neither you nor Burke survived the expedition.'

'What! That's terrible news,' exclaimed Wills. 'I've got a pretty girl waiting for me when I get home. Just wait 'til Burke gets back. I'll give him a piece of my mind. He promised me!'

Harry and Larry looked at each other in bewilderment.

'Don't worry,' said Larry. 'I'm sure you'll get home again.'

'Sorry, boys. Got to go. I feel so tired. My arms and legs feel almost paralysed. Can only walk a few yards before the muscle cramps stop me in my tracks. Just the exertion of getting up induces an indescribable sensation of pain and helplessness.'

'It was the toxins from those roots you cooked up,' explained Harry. 'They say you didn't cook them long enough.'

'By Jove!' exclaimed Wills. 'I think you're right. I kept telling Burke they tasted bitter. Just wait 'til the old boy returns. Thanks for the tip. Gosh, I feel so tired. Best head inside for another nap. See you later, boys.'

'See ya, Wills,' said Harry.

The ghost of Wills disappeared back into the tree.

Larry felt a heaviness wash over his body. 'Poor soul,' he uttered. 'Doesn't know he's dead.'

There was no reply except for a distant snoring. The Mice giggled.

'Hey,' said Harry, his ears perking up alert. 'Remember what Merlin the Owl said to us. "There are a few special beings in life that think outside the box of normality. Innovators. Explorers." Burke and Wills were Explorers. I wonder if Merlin would call them Way Show-ers too?'

'Of course,' said Larry. 'Explorers who were willing to take a risk to make a difference ... except they didn't make it.'

'I wonder what Virtues they had that made them such keen Explorers?' asked Harry.

'I guess Courage and Hope, would be a good start,' replied Larry. He thought about their own explorations. Certainly, they showed Courage to fight off the Sea Eagle chicks, but wasn't that just a survival instinct? He shrugged his shoulders. And what about Hope? Black Jack, the Red-tailed Cockatoo, lived in Hope that humans would change their ways to stop the demise of the Great Barrier Reef. Corey, the Cassowary, lived in Hope that the Daintree would survive! But apart from wanting to return to the Bunyas, Larry didn't really have any idea what Hope was about. His thoughts were suddenly interrupted by Mrs H's call. They scampered back to the Toyota.

'Time to roll!' shouted Izzy, directing her gaze towards her husband in the distance.

Charlie was on his hands and knees, taking a photo. The strange lizard was frozen still, its neck projecting a display of magnificent colourful frills. ''Hold on, Izzy. I'm coming.' shouted Charlie. 'Just one more camera shot.'

The Toyota burst into life. Charlie jumped in surprise. Frantically, he grabbed his camera gear and ran back towards the 4WD.

As the Toyota pulled out of the campsite, Harry looked back to see a ghostly figure waving goodbye. 'Spooky,' he mumbled.

Soon they were back on the red, red road with a cloud of dust billowing behind them, pondering the Balance of Life.

Larry's did you know...

In 1859 the South Australian government offered a prize for the first expedition to cross Australia from South to North. Irish born Policeman Robert O'Hara Burke, led an expedition organised by the Victorian Exploration Committee, which included William John Wills, who was the expedition's surveyor and astronomer.

Burke set off on August the 20th 1960, with 18 other people, including 6 Irishmen, 5 Englishmen, 3 Germans, and an American. This was the first expedition to use camels as a means of transport. The 26 camels were looked after by the 3 Afghan and

1 Indian Camel drivers. Burke also took 23 horses and 6 wagons to carry the 2 tonnes of equipment, various bits of furniture and a supply of food for two years. Unfortunately, they had to dump a lot of gear and 60 gallons of rum as three of the wagons broke down after the first day. The expedition arrived at Coopers Creek, named camp 63, on November the 11th, at the southern edge of the Strezlecki Desert.

Determined to make it to the Gulf, Burke, Wills and two of his men, set out from Camp 75 to travel the final leg of their expedition, leaving the other men to wait 3 months for their return. Unfortunately, it took them eight weeks to get from Coopers Creek to camp 119, just south of the Gulf of Carpentaria. Burke and Wills set off by themselves to reach the Gulf, but they failed to see the sea, because mud and thick mangrove swamps blocked their path.

After dealing with monsoon rains and dysentery, they finally returned to Coopers Creek on the 21st of April. Burke, Wills and King, the other remaining man, found that the other party of men, who had been waiting for almost five months, had left, just nine hours before. Some food had been left in a box buried at the base of a tree, with a sign saying DIG.

By now Burke, Wills and King were very sick and starving. Burke died of starvation and suspected toxins from under-cooked bush tucker on July 1, 1861. Wills died a few days later. After burying Wills, King joined the Yantruwanta people, who looked after him until he was found on September 15, 1861 by other explorers.

CHAPTER FOUR

The Road Less Travelled

★

Charlie had stopped the Toyota to admire the black lava rocks lining the creek bed.

'Gotta check these rocks out,' said Charlie. 'I wonder where this lava flow came from?'

'We're hundreds of miles from Undara,' replied Izzy, remembering the guide explaining how the lava flow had travelled about 100 km from the original Volcano eruption site.

Izzy and Charlie jumped out to investigate.

Meanwhile, Harry and Larry were more concerned with the strange bird standing to the left side of the 4WD. They scrambled down the side of the Toyota to get a closer look.

'Hey Fellas!' cried the tall lanky Bird. 'You's lost?'

It was a large, grey feathered bird with very long legs. Its tall curved neck was connected to a very pointy beak. Its head was striped with a red band, like a superhero mask.

'What ya looking at, Boy'os,' cried the Bird. 'Spit it out. Come on. Haven't got all day, you know.'

'Are you a Stork?' asked Harry.

'Hey! Watch the language!' yelled the Bird. 'I'm no Stork, mate. Come on! You think I'm some sort of commoner?'

'Sorry, Mr Bird,' apologised Larry, 'but we're not from here, so we're very puzzled by your appearance.'

'Well, now,' replied the Bird. 'That's a better response. Not like your rude friend here. No idea! The cheek of it, calling me a Stork.'

'So, what sort of Bird are you?' asked Larry.

'The most regal kind,' exclaimed the Bird. 'Dashing. Very talented.'

'Talented?' asked Harry.

'Yes. Very talented, I must say,' declared the Bird. 'Best dancer in Leichardt Falls. Gold medal standard, if you know what I mean.'

'Dancer?' questioned Harry, puzzled by the strange conversation.

'Yes, Dancer,' replied the Bird. 'You know, Foxtrot, Tango, Waltz. You name it. I'm the best! Just ask my wife.'

The Bird waltzed gracefully through the water, his legs flexing effortlessly.

'Yes, I see,' said Larry. 'So, what species of Bird are you?'

'Ah! Now you pinned me down, cheeky rascal,' replied the Bird. 'Yes, ok. Got me this time. Dancing Queen I am.'

'It says here, you're a Brolga,' stated Larry, looking at Mr H's Australian Birds guide book.

'Ha! Got me!' the Brolga said. 'Lucky guess. Nailed it. Well done, you little Smarty Pants.'

Larry was puzzled. He'd never met a character like this before. The Animals and Birds in the Bunyas never talked like this. And they certainly hadn't come across one as strange on their travels so far.

'Smarty Pants?' said Harry, feeling annoyed at the Brolga's comments. 'That's a bit rude, don't you think? We're brave Mouseketeers from the Bunya mountains. Merlin the Owl said we were Way Show-ers!'

'See! That proves it! Show-offs!' replied the Brolga. 'Don't see me prancing around saying I'm a Way Show-er!'

'Hey!' cried Larry. 'That's not fair! It's alright for you to ...'

'Zip it, Mouse Brain,' said the Brolga. 'I've got the Gold Medal three years straight! Beat that, you little Smarty Pants.'

'But ...' Harry was about to stand up for his little brother, but he was knocked off-balance as the Brolga spread his wings.

'Whoops,' continued the Brolga, looking skyward. 'Here comes the Missus.'

High in the sky the Mice could see a giant Bird,

her wings spread wide, as she glided effortlessly across the sky.

'Must get going. Can't talk to the Plebs,' he rambled. 'Get into trouble. Must go. Gotta get my dancing shoes on!'

Mr Brolga spread his giant wings and ran across the top of the water until he gained momentum to fly. His outstretched wings pumped the air, slowly lifting him higher, as he flew in a long swooping arc, up towards the clouds. After several minutes, he finally joined Mrs Brolga, and together they flew westwards.

'Quite a talker,' grumbled Harry. 'How rude was he!'

'He was the most arrogant Bird I have ever met,' stated Larry. 'I guess not everyone is willing to listen.' Larry drifted back to the conversation with Merlin. *The key to the integration of Human and Animal Kingdoms is the willingness to listen. How can we change the world if we are not willing to hear and respect each other?* His thought process was interrupted by the return of Mr and Mrs H.

'Right'o, you lot!' said Charlie. 'Onwards and upwards!' The Toyota roared to life, and they continued up the road. A little further, a sign pointed to Leichardt Falls. Charlie parked the 4WD on the side of the road, and they all jumped out and walked over towards the rocky embankment. Only then did the view reveal the beauty of a series of cascading waterfalls plummeting into a large catchment of water.

'Check out the sign!' stated Harry. 'It says "beware of Crocs below the falls".'

'Ewwwweeee,' squealed Larry, looking into the muddy brown water below. He couldn't see the bottom, let alone any Crocs lurking around.

'Race you to the falls,' cried Harry.

'Careful, boys!' shouted Izzy, but it was too late. They were gone, running and skipping over the rocks, towards the falls.

'I guess they need to let off a bit of steam,' said Charlie. 'It's been a long day driving on those red, dusty roads.'

'Me too!' laughed Izzy, and she danced over the rocks to the falls.

Izzy gazed dreamily into the gushing water before it disappeared over the edge of the waterfall, allowing the cold water to sooth her feet and wash away the ingrained red dirt of the outback. Sparkles of sunlight danced in the swirling water currents, gurgling and bubbling. It reminded her of her childhood, looking for fairies, a favourite playtime game, when imagination and reality blended as one. She remembered her love for Nature, spending hours wistfully lost in the depths of time. The Outback rekindled that memory. The red dirt and rugged landscape sung to her soul. It felt like home.

Meanwhile, Harry and Larry had been chasing each other around the rocks, jumping over the little spouts of water as they played tag. Larry stopped to collect his breath. He looked over to Mrs H, who was sitting on a rock dangling her feet in the water singing a gentle tune. Larry smiled to himself. There was hope for humans after all.

As if a giant wind swept through, a huge flock of Red Tailed Black Cockatoos flew into the tall gum trees near the waterfall. Izzy looked up into the giant Eucalypts and watched the glossy black Birds spread their wings as they gently landed on the upper-most branches, showing the brilliant red and orange strips in their tail feathers. As the flock settled amongst the branches, they started to squabble amongst themselves.

'Hey Mabel! Wanna come share my branch for the night?'

'Not very likely, George.'

'That's not very nice,' squawked Ethel, 'hurting the young boy's feelings like that.'

'Don't worry, Darling,' replied Percy. 'Plenty of other young females for him to harass.'

'Hey look down there,' cried George. 'Two Mice dressed in safari suits, like miniature humans. Isn't that a scream!'

'Aren't they the Mice everyone's been talking about from the Cockatoo Telegraph?' shrieked Mabel.

'I heard Merlin the Wise had called them the Way Show-ers,' replied Ethel. 'They may be the Chosen Ones, who will help humans relearn how to communicate with the Animal Kingdom.'

'Fat chance of that!' laughed George. 'Those humans are just stupid, ignorant beings!'

Izzy looked up in surprize at the squabbling Cockatoos. 'Hey!' she cried. 'I heard that!

George, the Cockatoo, froze silent, and looked around to see who was speaking.

'Yes, you, Big Beak!' shouted Izzy, standing up and waving. 'I understood every word you said. Merlin the Wise said he was honoured to meet us too, and he definitely didn't call me stupid.'

'Ha ha, Big Beak!' squawked Percy. 'Could have told ya to put a peg on it.'

George gulped. 'Sorry, Madam. I didn't realise.' He was so embarrassed, he took flight towards the sun.

'I'm so sorry, Mrs Human,' said Ethel. 'The young boys in our flock have a lot to learn, particularly with respect towards humans. I've heard so much about you all, and very honoured to speak to you in person.'

'Thank you, Mrs Cockatoo,' replied Izzy. 'I hope that young Bird learnt his lesson.'

Harry and Larry stopped in surprize, their mouths wide open.

'Did Mrs H just give that Bird a serve?' asked Larry.

'Glad they didn't call us the stupid ones this time,' said Harry. He remembered the remarks from Red Eye, one of the Black Red-tailed Cockatoos from Yeppoon, who had called them stupid bush Mice. 'Bet Mrs H will make headlines on the Cockatoo Telegraph!'

The Mice laughed.

Meanwhile, the sun was gently sinking towards the horizon. Charlie suddenly realised their predicament. 'Oops,' cried Charlie. 'Time to go.' 'Glad we're not camping here,' added Izzy. 'Had enough of those cheeky Cockatoos.'

With the two Mice on board, Charlie fired up the engine and headed down the road towards Burketown.

'Should get there at dusk,' said Charlie. 'Fifty kilometres to go. Easy peasey!'

As they rattled down the corrugated dirt road, a group of giant Cows with single humps blocked the road.

'Out of the way,' shouted Charlie.

'Easy,' whispered Izzy. 'Don't want to upset the one with the horns.'

'Hey! Who do you think you are, driving through here,' bellowed the Bull. 'This is our bedtime.'

The Mice jumped up on the dashboard.

'What!' cried Harry. 'You can't sleep here. This is a road.'

'Who cares what you think,' exclaimed the Bull. 'Warmest place for my old bones. Have a little respect for your Elders.'

'Might have to drive around that one, Mr H,' whispered Harry. 'He's not going to budge.'

Kilometre after kilometre, herds of Cattle criss-crossed the roads, some already kneeling in their sleeping positions.

'Watch out,' cried Izzy, grabbing the dashboard.

A huge Kangaroo jumped past the bumper bar.

'Phew! That was close,' exclaimed Charlie.

'Here comes another,' shouted Larry.

Charlie idled along slowly, dodging Cows and Roos from all sides of the car.

'I dare say, this is not the best time to drive in these parts,' he said.

'Just take it easy,' suggested Izzy, 'and don't hit any of those Animals.'

'Certainly not one of those talking Cows,' laughed Charlie.

Finally, they rocked up to the Burketown Caravan Park, two hours after leaving Leichardt Falls.

Charlie stumbled into the office.

'Wondering if you'd get here?' exclaimed the Caretaker. 'Just about to lock up.'

'Lucky for us,' yawned Charlie. 'Didn't think we'd make it.'

'Looks like a hot shower and bed for you lot,' she replied. 'Tell ya what. How 'bout you settle up in the morning. I see you need the rest.'

'Cheers,' said Charlie, as he stumbled back to the car.

An hour later, they were all fast asleep in the Humbledink campsite, dreaming of Cows and Roos.

Larry's did you know...

For 50,000 years, traditional owners, the Gangalidda Garawa and the Waanyi people have inhabited the rich hunting habitats of this region.

By the beginning of the 17th century the Dutch East India Company was well established in the East Indies and was looking to extend its influence.

Willem Janz sailed south to the gulf of Carpentaria in 1606.

Jan Carstensz landed in several spots along the eastern side of the Gulf in 1623.

Abel Tasman traversed the north coast in 1644.

In 1802-3 Matthew Flinders, for the British, charted the Gulf coast in response to Dutch and French interests.

1841 John Stokes aboard "The Beagle" praised the Burketown region's "Plains of Promise" for future cattle grazing.

CHAPTER FIVE

Lost City

'I just love the Outback,' said Izzy, rubbing the back of her neck 'but I could do with a back and neck massage.'

'Me too,' cried Charlie.

They were rumbling down the road into Limmen National Park, just north of the mining town of Boorooloola, on the edge of the Gulf. The road was rough with corrugations, dispersed with patches of deep, sandy trenches. Charlie's eyes were peeled to the road to ensure they didn't hit a hidden rut, but the road was like a field of land mines. Izzy winched in pain every time Charlie hit a sand rut, causing the 4WD to violently bounce around.

A road sign pointed to the Southern Lost City: 4 kilometres.

'That looks like a great place to set up camp,' suggested Charlie. 'The photos in the brochure look amazing.'

As they drove up the sandy track towards the campsite, the great pillars appeared before them.

'Wow!' cried Harry. 'That does look like tall buildings of a city, lost in time.'

'Almost spooky,' replied Larry.

'Wouldn't want to get lost in there,' said Charlie.

After they all helped set up camp, Charlie and the Mice prepared to go off hiking amongst the pillars.

'Back soon, Darling,' called Charlie.

'Make sure you're back before dark,' cautioned Izzy.

'Of course,' answered Charlie. 'You know me.'

'Hmmmm,' muttered Izzy.

'Ok, boys!' said Charlie. 'The sign says the circuit

track is only two and a half kilometres. Shouldn't take long.'

'Heard that one before?' laughed Harry.

They headed along the track, which wove in and around the giant pillars that towered above them.

'Wow!' cried Charlie, marvelling at the different colours and patterns in the rocks. 'Look at the layers of sand.'

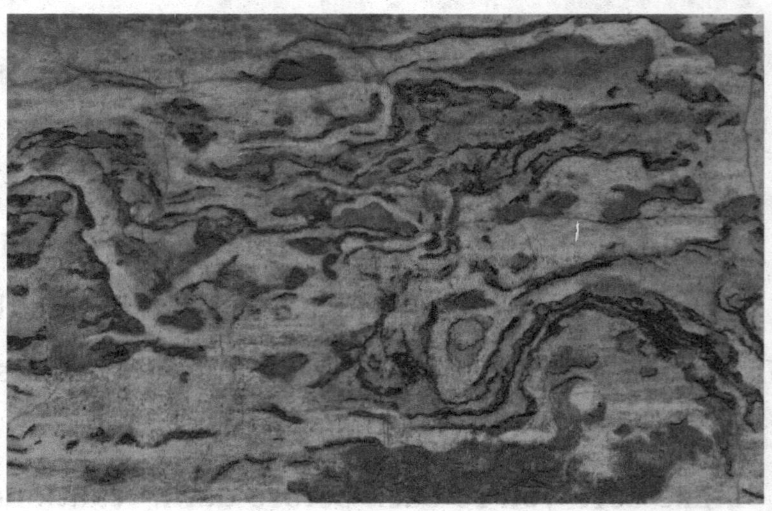

'Mrs Google says they're part of an ancient seabed formed 1500 million years ago,' replied Larry.

'Wow!' said Harry, 'that's way older than those rocks on Dunk Island.'

As they continued walking, Harry and Larry ran among the pillars playing hide and seek, whilst Charlie took hundreds of photos. The late afternoon sun created beautiful shadows in the rocks and accentuated the redness in the mineral encased sandstone. As they reached the ridgeline, the sun was setting, creating a warm red glow across the mountains.

'Just beautiful, eh boys,' contemplated Charlie. 'Doesn't get better than this.'

'Awesome,' cried Harry.

'Didn't we say to Mrs H, that we would be back before dark?' reminded Larry.

'Oh, yes,' replied Charlie. 'Just a few more shots and we'll head off.'

Another twenty photos later, the Mice and Charlie headed off down the track towards the campsite. The track was marked using blue arrows that helped indicate the stony path. As they walked through one group of the giant pillars, footprints led off in three different directions.

'Hey,' queried Charlie. 'Can you see any more blue markers?'

'Got me puzzled,' replied Harry.

The Mice jumped down and helped Charlie search for the missing marker. Charlie even went back to the last set of markers to see if they had come the wrong way. They continued walking around in circles but there was no sign of an obvious track.

Charlie looked up at the sky. There was a distant pale light on the horizon as the darkness crept in. There were no stars visible but it was getting close. 'Oops,' he muttered, as he checked his pockets for a torch light.

'Ok, boys, forgot the torch.' he said aloud. 'We have two choices. We either keep going and hope that we find the track again, or we go back via the way we came in.'

'Either way, we'll be walking back in the dark,' calculated Harry.

'Best we go back the way we came,' suggested Larry. 'At least we have the track to follow so we won't get lost.'

'Hopefully not,' replied Charlie. 'Looks like it's the long way home.'

They headed up the ridge in good spirits, and started to walk back down towards the pillars. By then the night sky had turned black, and the stars had come out to play. Unfortunately, there was no moon to light their way. The looming shadows of the giant pillars disappeared into the night, and the blue markers that marked the track disappeared from Charlie's vision. It was so dark that he couldn't see anything in front of him, as he shuffled his feet along the stony path.

'Ouch,' he cried, as he stubbed his toe on a rock. He tried lifting his feet high, in a very silly manner, so he wouldn't hurt his toes again, but again he stubbed his toe. Charlie stopped to have a breather.

'Hey, Mr H,' called Harry. 'Did you know Mice have very good night vision? We could lead you along the track.'

'Yeah,' added Larry. 'We could attach some ropes

to your hands and lead you along the path.'

'I suppose so,' replied Charlie. 'I can't see a thing in front of me, and I keep stubbing my toes.'

Charlie set down his pack, so the Mice could retrieve their climbing ropes that they had stored away for emergencies. They secured a rope to each of Charlie's hands and positioned themselves in front of him.

'Ok, Mr H,' ordered Harry. 'When I pull on the rope linked to your left hand, you move your left foot forward.'

'And the same with the right hand,' added Larry.

'Roger that,' replied Charlie. 'I'm all yours.'

'Ok, Mr H,' commanded Larry. 'Move your right foot forward.'

'And now your left foot,' called Harry.

It was very slow and awkward but they continued down the track, one step at a time. Charlie continued to stub his toes on rocks and stumps.

Suddenly there was a rustling in the bushes next to him. Charlie jumped in fright.

'What was that?' he yelled.

'I am that,' said a small husky Voice.

'Who is that?' asked Harry, moving closer to the rustling.

'That is I,' answered the Voice.

'Hi, that is I,' replied Harry. 'Who are you?'

'I am me, that's who I am. With a ring in my tail, I swing when I can.'

'Ah ha! You must be a Possum,' called out Larry, relieved to know it wasn't a Snake. 'We are bush Mice from the Bunya Mountains. I'm Larry and this is my brother Harry.'

'Bush Mice he says, that he would, a Larry and Harry, from the Mountainhood.'

'And do you live here?' asked Harry.

'I live here, I live there. Live I do, everywhere,' replied the Possum.

'We were heading back to our camp, when it got dark,' explained Larry. 'Now it's so difficult to see.'

'See I do, so easily. Dark is dark, if one can't see.'

'I can't see a thing in the dark,' said Charlie.

'Dark is a thing, if one can't see. If only the dark, could not be.'

'How do you see in the dark?' asked Charlie.

'How to see? How to see? See with eyes, is not to be. See with nose, is easy to me. See with mind, is harder to be,' sang the Possum.

'See with mind?' asked Charlie. 'Sounds simple, but can you really?'

'Simple do, and simple be. Trust and Faith, is much more free.'

'Trust and Faith that I won't kick another rock,' said Charlie. 'You've got to be joking.'

'Joke not me, if you want to see. Simple be, and Trust all three.'

'I get it!' cried Larry. 'We need to work together, with Trust and Faith.'

'Trust me not, be trouble near. Faith when pure, will get you there.'

'I know what to do,' cried Larry, hopping about.

'You do?' asked Charlie, still confused.

'Close your eyes, with listening mind. Trust your feet, you'll be fine,' sang the Possum again.

'I sort of get it,' said Charlie. 'but what do you mean by 'trust your feet?'

There was silence in the bushes. Their friend had disappeared.

'Thank you, Mr Possum,' called Larry, 'wherever you are.'

'He reminds me of Yoda,' laughed Charlie, 'from Star Wars.'

'Yeah' replied Harry. 'We've seen the movie too!'

'What,' gasped Charlie. 'Get out of here. That's so funny. Mice watching human movies.'

'Ok, guys. Let's focus here,' stated Larry. 'We need to use our minds to get us home safely.'

Charlie took a deep breath and closed his eyes. After a few moments, he relaxed and allowed the boys to direct his steps with ease. He listened to the sounds of the ground under his feet, and felt the air around him so he could feel how close he was to the rock walls. He smelt the fragrance of the trees, as he brushed past them, and saw within his mind the path they had travelled before.

Soon they arrived home, laughing and singing up the final path to the campsite.

'Glad you're home,' exclaimed Izzy. 'Something told me that you were safe.'

'Thanks to our Possum friend, Mr Yoda,' replied Charlie, 'the path was made clear.'

'Clear to see, and here we be,' sang Larry.

And they all laughed, as they headed inside for dinner.

Larry's did you know...

Limmen National Park is about 275 Kms from Katherine. It is an isolated park featuring spectacular and ancient sandstone pillars formed by erosion over millions of years.

The giant sandstone pillars are part of an ancient seabed formed 1500 million years ago. Over the years, water and wind have carved these incredible shapes. The varied colours are due to the mineral composition of the sandstone. The very dark colours are usually created by moss or algae that rarely see direct sun. The algae grew through deposited sediments on an ancient seabed, forming Stromatolites. They date back as far as 3.5 billion years.

CHAPTER SIX

The Monster of Butterfly Springs

'Five degrees to Starboard,' commanded Harry.

Larry paddled on the left side as the canoe glided smoothly across the tea-tree stained water towards the cliff wall of the Billabong.

After leaving the amazing pillared rocks at Southern Lost City, they had decided to explore another campsite in Limmen National Park, only a few kilometres up the road. The campsite was situated next to a beautiful billabong, fed by a gentle waterfall that trickled down the rock wall. Mrs H had perfected her boat building skills and created a new craft, a canoe, which the boys named 'HMAS Esmeralda'.

'How's the canoe going?' called out Izzy.

'Magnificent,' yelled Harry. He scanned the bottom of the canoe where Mrs H had woven paperbark into the spear grass matting to make it waterproof. 'Not a sign of any leaks.'

Meanwhile Charlie was chasing Butterflies with his camera. 'Come over here, Darling. Check out this spotted white one!'

Harry and Larry continued to paddle across the vast billabong.

Suddenly from the murky shadows, a dark shape slithered towards them.

'Hey, Harry! What's that? Fifteen degrees towards

starboard. Is it a Fish? An Eel?'

'No, it's a Snake!' cried Harry, as he recognised the S-like shape and movement of its body gliding across the water. He was well aware of how dangerous Snakes were, as they'd had a few close counters with a Red-bellied Black Snake called Bluey, as well as other members in his gang. A Snake is a Snake, whether venomous or not, and their diet includes MICE!

The eyes of the Snake gleamed in the sunlight, as it slithered across the top of the water, straight towards their little canoe.

'Watch out!' yelled Larry. 'Paddle for your life!'

Harry and Larry were splashing around in a panic, going nowhere fast.

The Snake's tongue flickered in and out, tasting the scent of the two Mice. It was a metre away from their canoe.

Larry looked back in horror to see the Snake open its mouth. 'We're gonners, Harry!'

Suddenly there was a giant splash, and the Mice

were nearly knocked out of the boat as it was rocked by the sudden waves.

'Hold on,' called Harry.

'Oh no, I've lost my oar!' cried Larry.

There was a stifled hiss from behind. The Mice froze, too scared to look behind them.

There was a gulp, followed by another. The silence was intense. Their hearts beat like cannon balls.

There was the sound of a huge burp. 'Oops, pardon me,' said a deep Voice.

Harry's eyebrows rose to the top of his head. He knew they were in trouble once again. His Mouse radar was jammed on panic, but his legs couldn't move.

'Been waiting for that Snake all day,' said the Voice. 'Sneaky little blighter!'

'P-p-pardon me,' stuttered Larry. He managed to unfreeze his body and turn towards the source of the Voice.

'Gulp!' Larry stared into a giant Dragon's eyes.

Harry, worried for the safety of his brother, turned around, and came eye to eye with the Loch Ness Monster of Butterfly Springs. 'Hey, don't you eat my brother! He's not very tasty!'

'Ho, ho, ho, ha, ha, ha, ho, ho, ho,' laughed the Monster. 'You two are the most humorous Mice I've ever met!'

'Yeah!' said Larry, feeling a bolt of courage surge within. 'And if you do something terrible to us, Mr and Mrs H will catch you and cut you open from your tongue to your tail, and get us out!'

'Ho, ho, ho, ha, ha, ha, ho, ho, ho,' laughed the Monster. 'I haven't had a good laugh like this for a long time! I like you two.'

'Like us to eat, or like us as friends?' asked Harry.

'Well said, my little Mousekin! My belly is full, so friends it must be!'

'Glad to meet you, Mr Dragon Monster. I'm Harry and this is Larry, my twin brother. We are sons of Mousolini Papa Mouse, leader of the Giant Stinging Tree clan, King of the Bunya tribes.'

The mention of their family lineage stirred Larry within, as he felt tears of moisture form in his eyes. Memories of his family and the loving warmth of Mama Mouse's hugs often surfaced when he was faced with his imminent death.

'Well indeed! Royal Mice! I should have guessed. I am Merten, the Water Monitor, King of Butterfly Springs. My ancestors from the time of the inland sea!'

'Yes, we saw the layers of sand in the red rock back in the Southern Lost City,' explained Larry.

'We Monitors originated from the time of the Dinosaurs, and the time before that, which they call Gondwana,' said Merten.

'That's impressive Mr Merten, Sir!' exclaimed Larry. 'Wilmar, Grandmother Whale, showed us a dream of Gondwana.'

'So, you're the two Mice they've been talking about on the Cockatoo Telegraph,' he said. 'Looks like I helped save your mission from a fatal ending.'

'We are truly thankful,' said Harry, contemplating

the nasty end to their adventures. 'Merlin the Owl said we need to understand certain Virtues before we get to read the Prophecy.'

'Well, if you ask me, that little Snake just scared the hebee jebees out of ya,' laughed Merten. 'You boys need to find a bit of Courage before you step out on this special mission.'

Larry's face turned white as a ghost. *My brother's the courageous one, not me*, he thought. *What's Courage got to do with it, if a hungry Snake, who's 100 times bigger than you, has you cornered?*

'Anyway, nice chatting with ya, but this old Dragon has to take back this meal for dinner. So long, King sons of the Bunyas!'

And in a flash, Merten sped to the other side of the water hole, launched himself out of the water, and scurried into the rocks.

'Wow!' cried Harry. 'He can move!'

'Yeah,' replied Larry, still thinking about his lack of Courage. 'Good thing we weren't on his menu'.

Harry and Larry searched for Mr and Mrs H who

had been oblivious to the Mice's deadly situation.

Mr H was photographing a Spotted Butterfly.

Meanwhile, Mrs H was chasing a blue Dragonfly.

Suddenly, she looked up and waved to the boys.

'Dinner time!' she called.

'I'm certainly hungry now,' remarked Harry.

'Me too,' replied Larry, as he grabbed a twig out of the water. 'Better start paddling.'

Larry's did you know...

The lifecycle of a butterfly starts with the female butterfly, who deposits her eggs onto a specific plant. The female has odour detectors which allow her to locate the plant, sometimes as far away as two or three kilometres.

Approximately four to five days after the fertilised egg has been laid, the caterpillar eats its way out of the shell. Caterpillars will grow and expand several times until the last stage.

The pupa or chrysalis is the final stage of the caterpillar where the metamorphosis takes place. This can take anywhere from one to four weeks in a tropical climate.

When the butterfly finally emerges, it pumps its wings to dry. Then it will fly off, ready to start the entire life cycle again. An average butterfly species has an adult life span of two weeks.

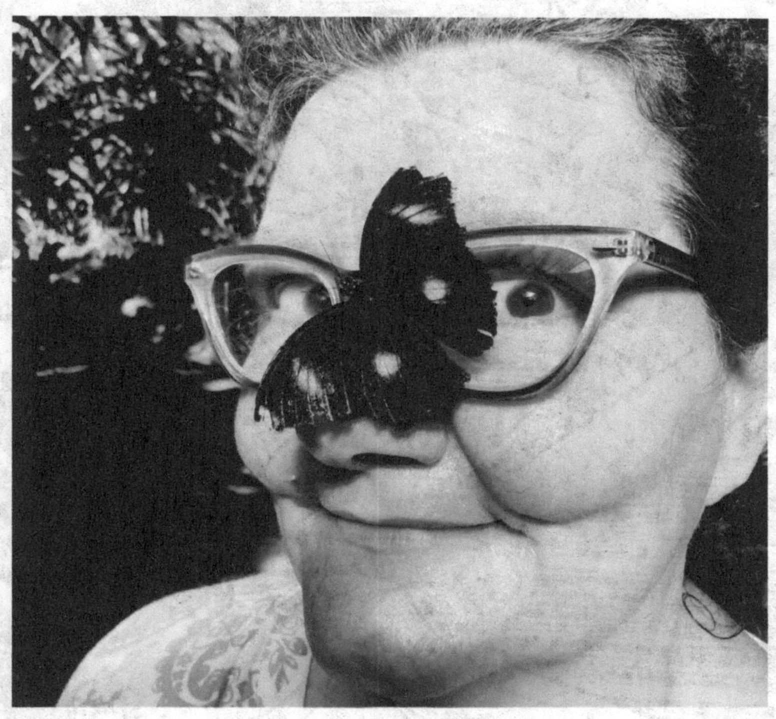

There are about 400 species of butterfly in Australia, mostly in the tropics.

A Butterfly survey conducted in Limen National Park, by Donald Franklin in July 2006, recorded 27 species.

CHAPTER SEVEN

Croc Country

★

Charlie Humbledink had hired a boat to go fishing on the Roper River, near Tomato Island. He was keen on catching one of the prize fishes of the area, a Barramundi. But they were not the only ones looking for a feed.

'So, what are you two doing in this neck of the woods?' said a deep Voice from the murky brown river.

The Mice looked up in horror.

'What's wrong, boys? Croc got your tongue? Ha, ha, ha, ha, ha,' said the Voice.

'Hey, you! Big Eyes? Keep away from our boat!' yelled Harry.

'Big Eyes eh? Have a look at my teeth.' The Croc

opened his jaws so wide that the Mice could see his gizzards.

Just then Charlie looked up. 'Holy Moly!' The shock of seeing those rows of ginormous sharp white teeth caused his legs to go like jelly. He had heard of stories of people being snatched by Crocs in the Territory, but to see one, face to face, was very scary indeed.

'Well, well, Sir. You look like a tasty treat, just waiting to jump into my jaws.'

Charlie's face turned white as a ghost. His life flashed before his eyes.

The Mice weren't so scared and were trying to poke Mr Croc with a stick to keep him away from the boat.

'Take that,' cried Harry, as he poked a stick into the Croc's right eye, with one of his fencing jabs.

'Ouch! Hey, that's not fair!' cried the Croc.

'Ha, ha, ha, Big Eyes!' laughed Larry. 'Who's the tough guy now?'

'I'll show you who's the tough guy!' The Croc

swung his tail hard against the boat sending the Mice flying towards the other side of the boat.

'Phew! That was close!' cried Harry.

There was a large splash and they turned around to see Mr H hanging off the side of the boat, his legs dangling in the air like antennas.

'Bingo!' shouted the Croc. 'Lunchtime!' He circled around the front of the boat, towards the helpless Charlie Humbledink.

Harry spied a bucket of old spark plugs near the outboard motor. 'Hey, Larry! Ammo!'

'Ripper!' cried Larry, and he grabbed his slingshot from his rucksack and handed it to his brother.

The Croc circled to the other side of the boat, only metres away from Charlie's dangling arms and body.

Harry picked out one of the spark plugs, placed it into position, then pulled back on the slingshot. 'Ready ... Steady ... Fire!' The spark plug flew through the air and hit the Croc in the left eye with a thud!

'Wowser!' cried the Croc. 'Hey, that smarts! I think you've blinded me!'

'Back off, Dinosaur Brain, or I'll let you have it again,' shouted Harry.

'What you call me? Dinosaur Brain! Watch out Fur Ball! You good for nothing vermin, black plague carriers, sleaze balls ...'

'Hey!' whispered Harry, signalling his brother 'Get Mr H into the boat, whilst we got this Croc flustered.'

'You Darn Rascals! I'll get you for this!' The old Croc was thrashing around in pain, hurtling insults at the Mice, unaware of the ruse to distract him and retrieve Charlie from his precarious position.

'Mr H!' whispered Larry, pulling his ears. 'Get up! Get up! You are in grave danger!'

'You Weasly Worms! Just you wait. I'll feed you to the Barras. You'll make a tasty treat! Nobody treats Caesar the Croc like this! Don't you know I am King of the Roper River?'

Meanwhile, Larry was able to alert Mr H and help him clamber back onto the fishing boat.

'Wow, that was stupid of me,' gasped Charlie.

'Didn't see that coming. Thanks Larry!'

'Hey! Where's my lunch? You measly little Vermin!' cried Caesar the Croc. 'Now you've got me angry! Taking my lunch away! Don't you know it's hard to get a decent feed these days?'

'Sure thing, Fat Head!' boasted Harry. 'Bring it on!'

'That's it! I'm coming in!'

'Watch out!' cried Larry.

The Croc barrelled full speed towards the boat with his jaws wide-open, razor sharp teeth gleaming in the sunlight.

Harry grabbed another spark plug, and pulled on the slingshot with all his might. 'Geronimo!' Harry let fly the slingshot, sending the spark plug spinning into the open jaws of the Croc. The spark plug landed a bullseye on the Croc's tonsils, sending him flying backwards in stinging pain.

'Waaaaaaaaaaaaa!' cried Caesar, landing hard on the river surface, with a huge sploosh, before he disappeared into the murky water.

'HOLY MOLEY,' cried Charlie. 'That was a ripper shot, Harry!'

'Nice one, brother!' added Larry, giving Harry a high five.

'Great teamwork,' said Harry. 'But the show's not over yet. He will be mad as hell and back for revenge.'

'Ok, men!' called out Larry. 'Choose your weapons!'

Larry had pulled out another slingshot, and found a packet of fishing weights. Harry joined five of the spark plugs together to make a Ninja Star. Charlie pulled out a grappling hook with a very pointy end. They tied themselves to the boat and waited patiently.

Suddenly there was a giant eruption as the Croc leaped out of the water.

'Fire!' cried Harry. They launched their weapons, striking the soft underbelly of the Croc.

'Ahhhhhhhh!' cried Caesar, as he plunged back into the water.

A giant wave rose metres in the air and engulfed

the boat, completely drenching Charlie and the two Mice. The boat rocked violently from side to side, but failed to capsize.

The Croc rose to the surface, still swearing and cursing, 'Crikey, that hurt. Despicable Rodents! You lot are asking for trouble!'

'Hey, Big Boy!' yelled Charlie. 'Don't be so hasty! My body is not as tasty as that fish those young bucks have caught, across the river, over there.'

The Croc turned to look over to the far side of the river, where a small boat with two young men were shouting with joy, having just caught a Barra on one of their lines. They were reeling it in slowly, with the Barra thrashing about in the water.

As quick as a flash, Caesar the Croc, King of the Roper River, sped towards the prized Barra in search of an easier meal.

'Wow, that was a close one,' cried Larry.

'Doesn't get closer than that,' added Harry.

'Truly thankful, boys! replied Charlie. 'I think you two Mice have shown great Courage to protect this old boy from that ginormous Croc!'

Larry realised he and his brother had risked their lives to save Mr H from the ferocious beast, without even thinking about their own death. Wow, he thought. Maybe I do have that Courage within me, after all.

'But not a word to Mrs H, or we'll be grounded for a month,' continued Charlie.

'Yes, Sir! Scout's Honour, Sir,' they answered.

'Don't know about you boys, but I've had enough excitement for one day. Time to head home for one of Mrs H's special hot chocolates.'

'Aye, aye, Captain!' cried Harry.

'Righto, boys! Start your engines!'

Larry's did you know...

Crocodiles have been around for 200 million years,

and are a descendant from the dinosaur age.

A large proportion of the coastal region of the Northern Territory, rich with mangroves and wetlands, is an ideal habitat for saltwater crocodiles. But they are also found along the coast of Queensland down to Mackay, and the northern part of Western Australia, including the Kimberley.

Saltwater crocs can grow to a very large size. Males can normally grow to 6 metres in length while females grow to around 3 metres in length. They have a 2nd eyelid, called a nictitating membrane which protects their eyes while underwater.

They have 64 to 68 teeth with a large fourth tooth, which is visible when they close their mouths.

They mostly eat fish, but are known to eat turtles, goannas, snakes, birds, livestock, and mud crabs.

Saltwater Crocodiles have been a protected species in Australia since 1971.

CHAPTER EIGHT
A Magical Journey

★

'Those cheeky Blighters!' cried Charlie.

The Humbledinks had set up camp, the night before, at a caravan park in the town of Mataranka, just south of Katherine in the Northern Territory. Charlie had woken from his deep sleep to the sounds of something moving around in their camping kitchen. Trying to put his trousers on quickly, he put his right foot through the fabric of his pants leg.

'Bloomin' Heck!' he cried.

'Keep the noise down, Charlie,' cried Izzy. 'You'll wake the neighbours with your bellowing.'

'Darn it, Izzy!' he ranted. 'I've ruined my favourite bush–walking trousers.'

'Patience, dear,' said Izzy. 'The critter won't have

time to eat all your muesli.'

Harry and Larry burst out laughing.

A startled furry face looked up at the commotion.

'Did someone say muesli?' asked the Critter.

'Not for sale!' cried Charlie quickly.

'Oh dear, it's a sweet little Wallaby,' cooed Izzy, looking out the bedroom window.

'Hello, Mr Wallaby,' said Larry.

'G'day,' replied the Wallaby. 'Someone mention muesli?'

'Sorry mate, but Mr H doesn't like to share his muesli ... with anyone!' answered Harry.

'Too right!' stated Charlie.

'That's a shame,' mumbled the Wallaby. 'Quite like a scrumptious muesli.'

'So, what's your name,' asked Larry.

'Wilbur,' he replied.

'Wilbur?' queried Harry. 'That's a strange name for a Wallaby.'

'Yes,' said Wilbur. 'Quite embarrassing actually. My mother named me after several of my grandparents. My full name is: Wilbur Gerard Ashton Henry Woolston.'

'Wow! That's a handle and a half,' exclaimed

Larry. My name is Larry and this is my brother Harry. And don't forget our human friends, Mr H and Mrs H.'

'G'day to you folks,' said Wilbur. 'So, if muesli is off the menu, what else have you got to eat?'

'Too early for breakfast, Wilbur, but you might get lucky later,' stated Charlie. 'Besides isn't it bad for your digestion to eat human food?'

'So, they keep telling me,' grumbled Wilbur. 'Guess I'd better hop along then. Site thirty-two has a couple of kind-hearted travellers. They serve a nice breakfast to starving Wallabies like me. So long, folks.' Wilbur hopped off in search of a promised land of treats.

'Guess you could say the grass is greener on the other side of the fence,' laughed Harry.

'All he could think about was his stomach!' exclaimed Larry.

'Reminds me of someone else I know,' called Izzy from the bedroom.

The Mice giggled, knowing they too, were often

ruled by their stomachs.

'Well, boys, while we're up, fancy a swim before breakfast?' asked Charlie. 'Those hot springs are pretty awesome I hear.'

'Sure thing, Mr H,' replied Harry.

'Can we take our canoe?' asked Larry.

'Why not!' cried Charlie, helping the Mice with the paddles and stringy bark-constructed canoe. 'Wanna come, Izzy?'

'No thanks. I feel I need to rest my aching bones,' she replied. 'You go enjoy yourselves!'

The Mice and Charlie jumped in the car and drove down the road to Bitter Springs. With their boat huddled under Charlie's arm, and the two Mice hanging onto the towel over his shoulder, they set off down to the creek. A thick layer of mist lay over the top of the water like frosting on a cake. Wisps of the mist drifted higher amongst the tall trunks of Livistonia Palms that lined the creek, carrying the scent of the rich mineral hot springs that bubbled up from the cracks further up the creek.

'What's that smell? Rotten eggs?' remarked Harry.

'Wasn't me!' exclaimed Charlie.

The Mice giggled, knowing how Charlie liked to blame anyone else but himself.

'Must be sulfur minerals in the water,' he added.

Charlie bent down and placed HMAS Esmerelda in the water as the Mice grabbed their paddles and hopped into their trusty canoe made by Mrs H, its hull made with woven reeds and lined with bark from the weeping paperbark trees. It was water tight.

'Harry, you're in the bow this time and I'll steer from the stern,' suggested Larry.

'Aye, aye, Captain,' replied Harry.

HMAS Esmeralda glided out into the middle of the creek. The Mice looked down into the crystal-clear waters at the submerged rocks and logs covered in emerald green moss and lichen, laying upon the sparkling white sand.

'Wow!' exclaimed Larry. 'Wish I'd brought my

goggles.'

The joyful moment was interrupted by Charlie's unceremonious water bomb, causing the canoe to rock and roll with the huge waves.

'Well, boys! What do you think? Beautiful, eh?' exclaimed Charlie.

'Yeah! Until your water bomb almost capsized our canoe,' complained Harry.

'Couldn't help myself,' laughed Charlie.

'I've lost my paddle again,' cried Larry, looking frantically around.

'There it is!' cried Charlie, spotting the coloured ice-cream stick paddle floating several meters further down the creek. 'Catch you in a bit.' Charlie swam casually down the stream, with his swimming pool noodle supporting his upper body, carried by the current. The Mice's canoe also floated gently down the creek.

'Forty-five degrees to starboard,' called Larry.

'Aye, aye, Captain,' answered Harry.

HMAS Esmeralda swung into the middle of the

crystalline creek. The waters glistened with emerald greens and sapphire blues. Larry lay on his back looking up at the sky, admiring the giant palm trees towering above them, their ladder like fronds drooping down towards the weeping paperbark trees that hung over the creek. A huge circular web spanned the over-hanging branches of the paperbarks. A large grey-bodied Spider, with long black legs, had spread-eagled itself in the middle of the web. This Golden Orb Spider was looking very serious. No hint of a smile.

'Hello,' called Larry, as they floated underneath the web.

'Don't bother me, I'm busy,' replied the Spider.

'Well,' said Harry. 'She's not very friendly.'

Meanwhile Harry had spotted a ripple in the water. He strained his eyes to see what was lurking under the water. 'All hands on deck,' he cried. 'Something's coming straight for our boat.'

Before Larry had a chance to move, a monstrous head with googly eyes shot out of the water.

'Hey! What are you two doing in my creek?' demanded the googly-eyed Creature.

'What?' cried Harry, shocked by the sudden outburst.

'Didn't you read the signs?' it continued.

'What signs?' answered Harry.

'Signs on the front gate of course. Can't you read?'

'R-read? Of c-course we c-can,' stuttered Larry.

'Well, maybe you should go back and read it,' ordered the Creature.

'What did it say, Googly Eyes?' asked Harry.

'"No Pets Allowed!"' stated the Creature.

'Pets?' asked Larry.

'Yes! No Pets, Dumbkoff! Are you deaf and blind?'

'We're nobody's Pet! Nor are we deaf, dumb or blind!' stated Harry, getting annoyed with the attitude of the Creature. 'Who do you think you are?'

'I'm Mildred, Chieftain of Short-necked Turtle Clan, Guardian of these waters.'

'That explains the grumpies,' whispered Harry.

'I heard that, Mouse Brain!' exclaimed Mildred. 'And who might you be?'

'I am Harry and this is my brother Larry. We are explorers from the Bunya Mountains; sons of Mousolini; leader of the Giant Stinging Tree clan; King of the Bunya tribes. Merlin, the Owl, called us the Way Show-ers.' Harry stuck out his chest with pride. Despite been so far away from home, he was a proud member of his Mousey tribe.

'Oh, my goodness,' exclaimed Mildred. 'I'm so sorry. I've heard about you from the Cockatoo Telegraph. My deepest apologies. It is an honour to meet you boys.'

'You may have thought we were Pets because we travel with our human caretakers, Mr and Mrs H. They, too, were honoured by Merlin, the Wise One.'

'Well, well,' said Mildred. 'First time I've heard Merlin speak with humans. Must go tell the council. Hey, King-sons! Wanna come for a ride?'

'Sure thing,' said Harry, who was up for anything.

'What about Mr H?' asked Larry.

'Oh, he'll be ok,' answered Mildred. 'We will send him a dream and I'll have someone watch over him.'

'Ok then,' replied Larry. 'Lead the way.'

'Firstly,' said Mildred. 'You need to eat some Willy Weed. It will help you breathe under water.'

Mildred suddenly disappeared, then reappeared with some green weed in her mouth. 'Chew on this, boys.'

The Mice grabbed the weed and began to chew.

'Blurp,' said Harry.

Bubbles of air, encased in sticky membranes, popped out of his mouth. Larry closed his mouth as a bubble was about to surface, and started to float.

'Right,' advised Mildred. 'Those bubbles are full of air and will help you breathe under water. Ready? Climb aboard!'

'Yes, Ma'am,' burped Larry.

Harry and Larry jumped on the soft neck of the Turtle, as she sank gently into the clear waters below. Harry tried to speak but blew bubbles in the water. Larry laughed, creating his own stream of bubbles. Harry grabbed one of the bigger bubbles and pressed it against his face until it encased his head. The water became instantly clear and he could see the reeds and rocks as clear as day. He gestured to Larry to do the same. Both the Mice marvelled at the underwater paradise they were entering. It was like a dream.

Gracefully, Mildred led them along the sandy bottom, waving to her children, as they passed. For a moment, the children were scared of the Mice upon the Chieftain's neck, but soon they were diving and weaving around them. Mildred dived deeper into a cavern, where tiny bubbles were rising from the cracks in the floor. Larry realized that this was the source of the thermal springs, one of many, that they saw. She took them through a deep cave at the bottom of the cavern, and they surfaced into an underground amphitheatre, where many Turtles were engaged in deep conversation.

'Hail, Oh Wise Council,' cried Mildred. 'I bring you some guests, whom Merlin the Wise calls the Way Show–ers.'

The Turtles turned in surprise at this address, and there was much whispering and chatter amongst them.

'Thank you, Chieftain Mildred,' replied an old Turtle, robed with a golden scarf.

'He looks like a Wise One,' whispered Harry.

'Blurp,' said Larry, who was still chewing on Willy Weed.

The old Turtle lumbered forward, fixing his googly eyes on the two Mice.

'Well, well, my friends,' said the Wise Turtle.

'It is not often we are honoured to meet with such young, gifted Mice. You must have made quite an impression on Mildred for her to bring you to this secret council.'

Harry reflected on their adventures and memorable events with the Wise Ones along their journey. 'We are young at heart,' replied Harry, 'and big on adventure. It is a surprise to be present at your council, too. It's not every day that Mice, such as ourselves, get to ride over the Great Barrier Reef on the wings of the great Red-tailed Black Cockatoos, reach into the depths of time with Wilmar, Grandmother of the Humpback Whales, and explore the clear crystal waters of Bitter Springs, breathing underwater by the magic of Willy Weed.'

'You certainly have had some amazing adventures, my young friends,' continued the old Turtle. 'There has been much discussion about your travels as relayed by the Cockatoo Telegraph. I guess time will tell whether you are the Chosen Ones they talk about in the Prophecy.'

'It is true that we have been told that we are the Chosen Ones, the Way Show-ers,' replied Larry. 'I have no idea what a Way Show-er is, let alone being Wise.' He remembered seeing Mrs H singing and dangling her feet in the water at Leichardt Falls, her face full of smiles and joy. 'But we have seen how our human friends, Mr and Mrs H, have enjoyed exploring the Outback, and connecting with Nature.' Larry laughed to himself, remembering how Mrs H had told off the young Red-tailed Cockatoo for calling her stupid. Then he realised that both Mr H and Mrs H now freely conversed with Animals, as predicted by Merlin the Wise. He remembered when they were caught out in the dark amongst the giant pillars at the Lost City. Mr H had learnt to see with his Mind, with the help of Yoda the Possum. He began to understand the miracles that had been happening during their Outback adventures. 'And our human friends have also learnt how to communicate with the Animal Kingdom, as Merlin had said would happen. Maybe the time is coming when our destiny will reveal itself,' he added.

'Well said, my little friend,' said the old Turtle. 'You have learnt many things, and encouraged your human friends to remember the old ways, reigniting the communication channels between humans and the Animal Kingdom. You have witnessed the willingness of your human friends to develop a deeper connection with Nature, and all that live upon Mother Earth. Not all will want to embrace these connections. And you have demonstrated some important Virtues, such as Courage, Respect and Wisdom, that are the foundation of those destined to be Way Show-ers.

The next stage of your mission is the Journey of the Heart. There lies a deeper understanding of your path. Good luck, my friends and may the voice of Inner Knowing be your guide.'

Suddenly the cavern started spinning. Everything became a blur. Harry and Larry lost consciousness; their minds went blank.

'Hey, boys,' called Charlie. 'I was wondering where you guys got to.' Charlie continued to drift down the stream with his swimming noodle tucked under his arms.

Harry opened his eyes. Their boat, HMAS Esmeralda, had got caught in one of the strands of the Golden Orb Spider's web, and was gently twirling in the current.'

'Larry! Are you awake?' he asked.

'Yeah, I'm here,' yawned Larry, stretching his arms. 'Was that for real or just a dream?'

'Not sure, mate, but at least we're safe,' replied Harry. He closed his eyes and tried to visualise the underground amphitheatre where the Turtle council addressed them. The words of the main Elder echoed in his mind. Your next mission is the Journey of the Heart. What did that mean? Merlin also mentioned the Path, and the opening of their Minds and Hearts. He had become more comfortable with being called the Chosen Ones, but there were more unanswered questions.

Larry, too, was lost in his thoughts, remembering their encounter with the wise Turtle Elder. Yes, he had witnessed the deeper connections that Izzy and Charlie were experiencing. But what part did that play in their path of the Chosen Ones? What is the mission? How does one have a Journey of the Heart? Larry's head hurt with all the questions that were whirling around in his head, but his thought processes were interrupted by Charlie's voice. 'Beautiful, isn't it? Someone said they saw a Turtle in the stream. Can't say I saw anything. Just my luck, eh boys?'

'Yes, Mr H,' replied Harry, winking at Larry.

'Well, I don't know about you guys, but I'm getting a little hungry,' said Charlie. 'How about we head home for breakfast?'

'Sure thing!' cried Harry, as he released them from the Spider's web, and started paddling down the creek.

'Me too, Mr H!' added Larry, pondering the next stage of their adventures, 'the Journey of the Heart', as they drifted down the stream together.

And so, the journey continues ...

Larry's did you know...

On the Stuart Highway, 106 km south of Katherine, lies the town of Mataranka, home of natural hot springs.

The thermal springs are fed by the ground water of the Georgina basin. The water from the springs has many minerals including Magnesium, Calcium, Sodium, and Sulphates. This produces a bitter taste in the water, and sometimes the Sulphide smell of rotten eggs.

(Bitter Springs Information board)

The flow of the water, averaging 30 million litres a day, creates a gentle current, enabling tourists to float down the 340 C stream.

The creek is lined by paperbark trees and ancient 'Livistona rigida' fan palms, linked back to Gondwana land. Many aquatic animals live in the creek, including Barramundi and Turtles.

ABOUT THE AUTHOR

David was born in New Zealand, but during a working holiday in Australia in 1984, he decided Australia was the place for him, and has lived here ever since. In early 2017, he and his wife moved to Tasmania, and settled in the beautiful Huon Valley with their two labradoodles. David is a podiatrist by trade, and enjoys bushwalking, photography, gardening, and bee keeping. His inspiration to write comes from his love for trees and wildlife, and his memories of childhood exploration. He includes a richness of history and culture in his writing that has come from extensive travels, both within Australia and overseas.

ABOUT THE ILLUSTRATOR

☆

M. K. PERRING

Growing up in England I loved reading and drawing! I was inspired by Roald Dahl, especially my favourite of his books 'The Witches', to keep making of creative stories and drawing interesting characters.

Moving to Australia was a huge culture shift for me, but I made new friends and kept being creative. I didn't always know what to pursue in life, but I had to create, I loved art. I studied films, animation, graphic design, illustrations. I became a jack of all trades!

It wasn't easy to follow my dreams, but I stayed positive, believed in myself, and listen to those who believed in me too.

Now, making beautiful illustrations and working with all kinds of authors is a dream come true, and only the start of my adventure.

BIBLIOGRAPHY

Chapter 1: Undara Volcanic National Park
https://en.wikipedia.org/wiki/Undara_Volcanic_National_Park

Chapter 2: Savannah Way
https://www.savannahway.com.au/destinations/gulf-savannah/

Chapter 3: Burke and Wills
https://en.wikipedia.org/wiki/Burke_and_Wills_expedition

Chapter 4: Early Explorers of the Gulf of Carpentaria
https://www.burke.qld.gov.au/our-region/history/a-brief-history-of-the-gulf-of-carpentaria

Chapter 5: Limmen National Park
From the Limmen National Park's information board at Southern Lost City

Chapter 6: Australian Butterflies
https://australianbutterflies.com/australian-butterfly-life-cycle/

Chapter 6: Australian Butterflies
https://library.dbca.wa.gov.au/static/FullTextFiles/072339.pdf

Chapter 7: Crocodiles
https://becrocwise.nt.gov.au/about-crocodiles/saltwater-crocodiles

Chapter 8: Mataranka Hot Springs/Bitter Springs National Park
https://www.bitterspringscabins.com.au/bitter-springs-thermal-pools.html

Don't miss the next exciting mis-adventures of Larry and Harry in book three available through Shawline Publishing.

Shawline Publishing Group Pty Ltd
www.shawlinepublishing.com.au